Tipsy and Mae Adventures

presents....

Tipsy and Mae Chase the Taco Tastes

Written and Illustrated by Kat Laxton

Copyright © 2022 Kat Laxton Ph.D.

All rights reserved.
No part of this book may be reproduced or used in any
manner without the prior written permission of the copyright owner,
except for the use of brief quotations in a book review.

To request permissions, contact the publisher at TipsyandMaeAdventures@gmail.com.
Paperback ISBN: 9798412722849

First paperback edition May 2022

All words, illustrations, cover art, layout and photographs by Kat Laxton Ph.D.

Printed by Kindle Direct Publishing in the USA

Kindle Direct Publishing
Monee, IL
kdp.amazon.com

Made in the USA

The following tale is based on true events...

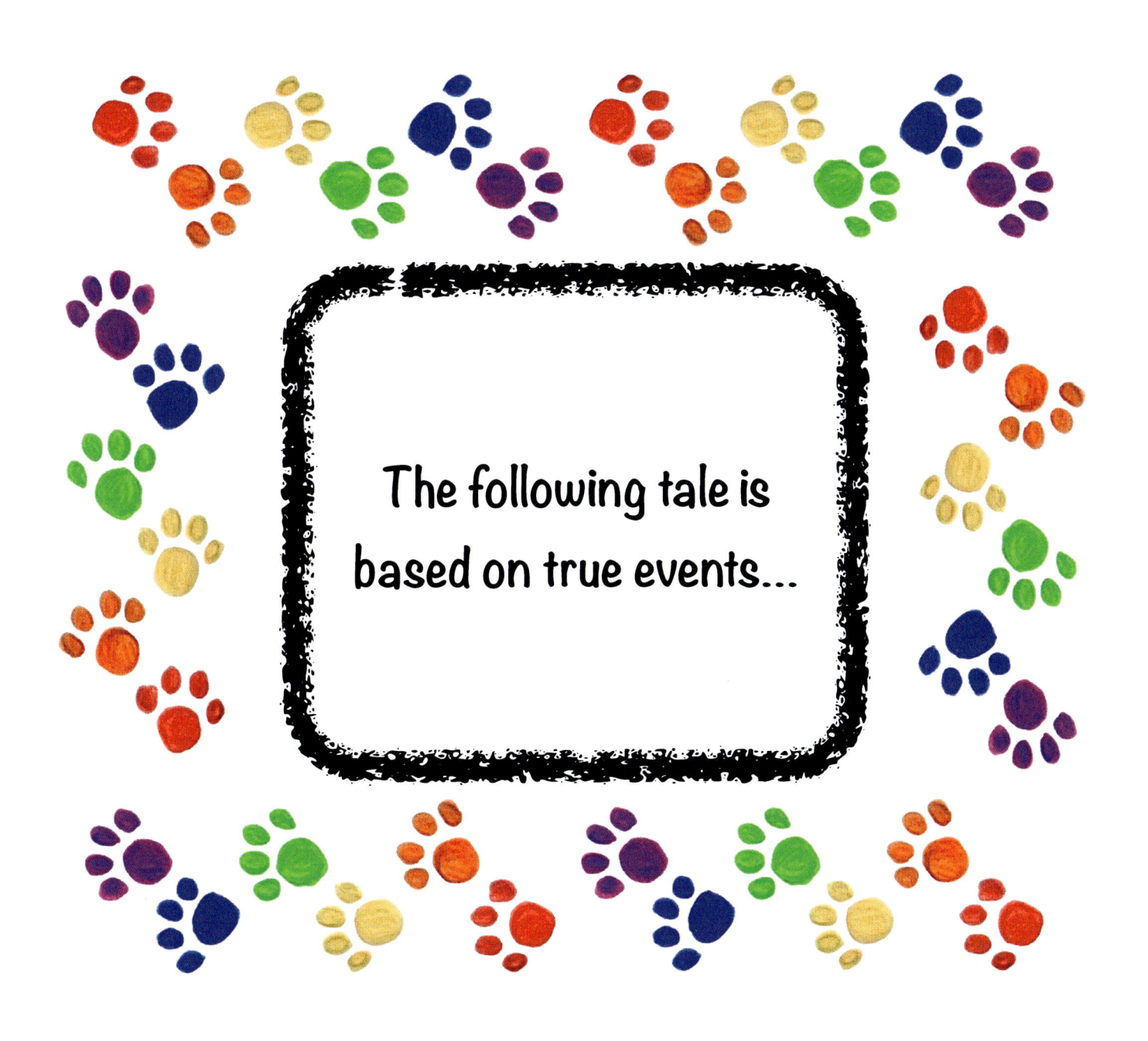

One afternoon
slumbering sounds filled the air,
when Tipsy woke abruptly
to loud gnawing on a chair.

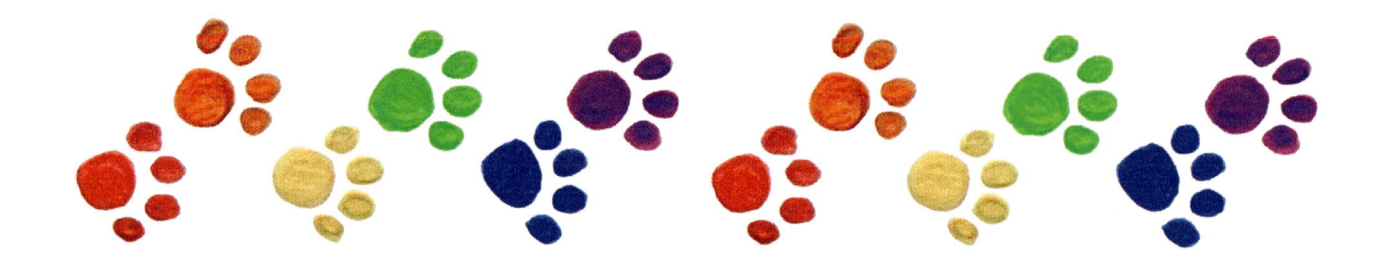

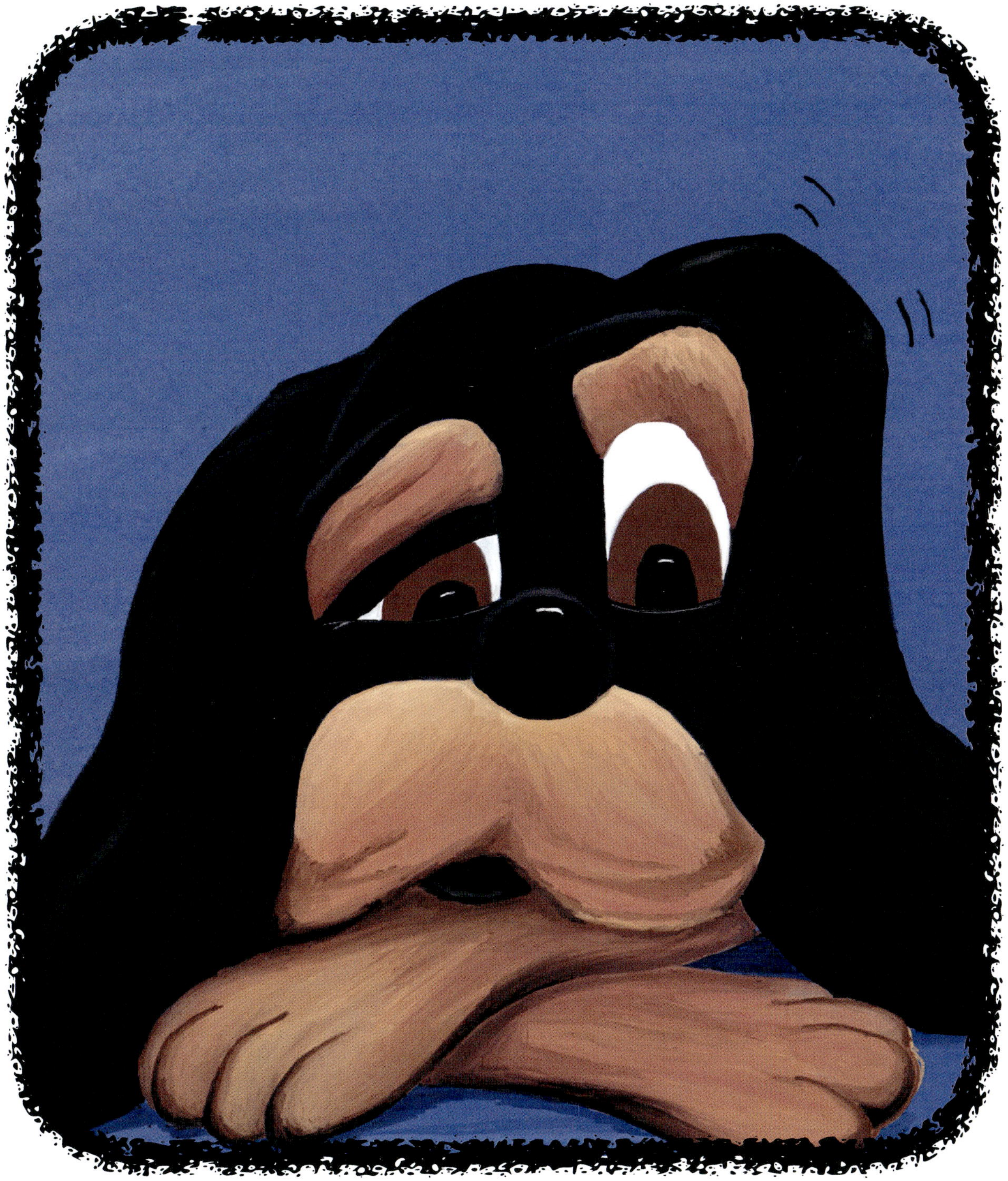

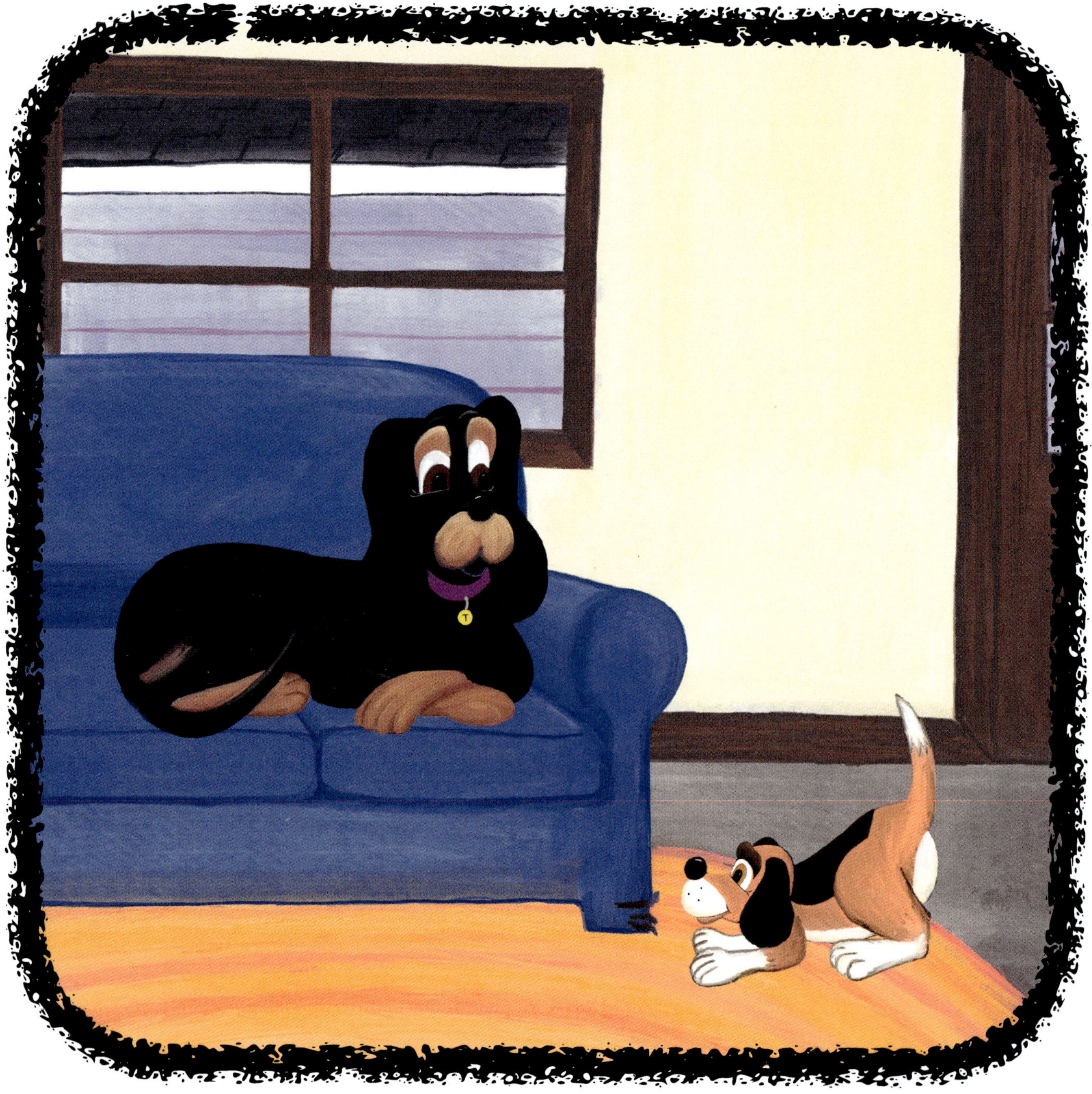

With surprise, Tipsy asked,
"what are you doing?"
Mae said, "I think it's obvious
that I am chewing."

"My stomach is empty
and I really need a snack.
This diet we've been put on
launched my hunger to attack!"

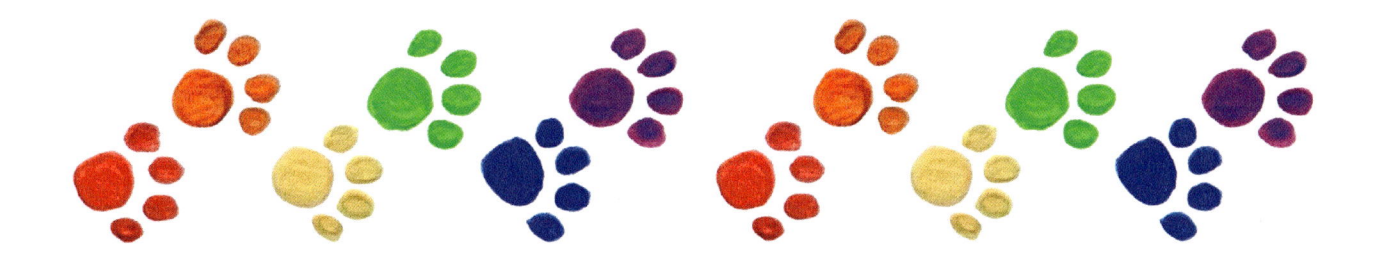

Well right at that moment
their noses got a whiff
of a delicious smell
that they could not resist.

They tucked their heads outside,
following the scent,
as a taco truck passed by,
smoke wafting out the vent.

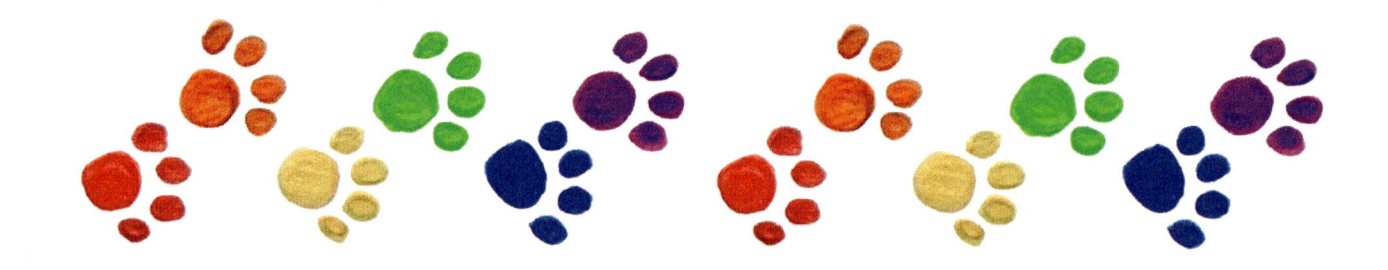

Mae said, "I need a taco! Let's follow that truck! But how to clear the fence? Fly over like a duck?"

Tipsy rolled her eyes while she walked to the fence. She nudged on a panel while Mae paced in suspense.

The panel wiggled over and there was just enough space for both dogs to fit through and chase the taco tastes!

While the space was tiny,
Tipsy slipped through with ease.
Unfortunately, Mae's belly
caused for a tight squeeze.

The beagle got her head in
but her shoulders had to shrug.
(Mae would've been stuck
without a helpful tug!)

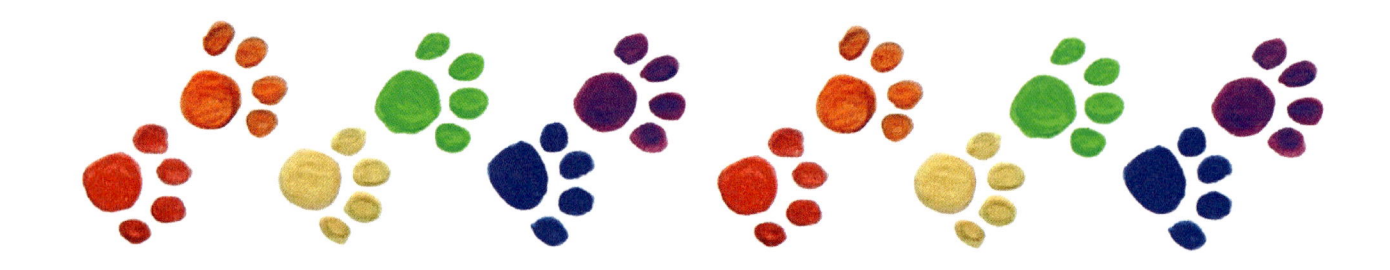

"Now follow that truck!" Mae howled in a riot.
Tipsy said, "I'm certain you're the reason
we were put on a diet!"

With stellar scenting skills
the hounds sniffed down the road.
The first thing they encountered
was a road-killed toad.

Tipsy said, "this toad smells amazing!
We've got such great luck!"
Mae said, "but it's not the same smells
as the taco truck!"

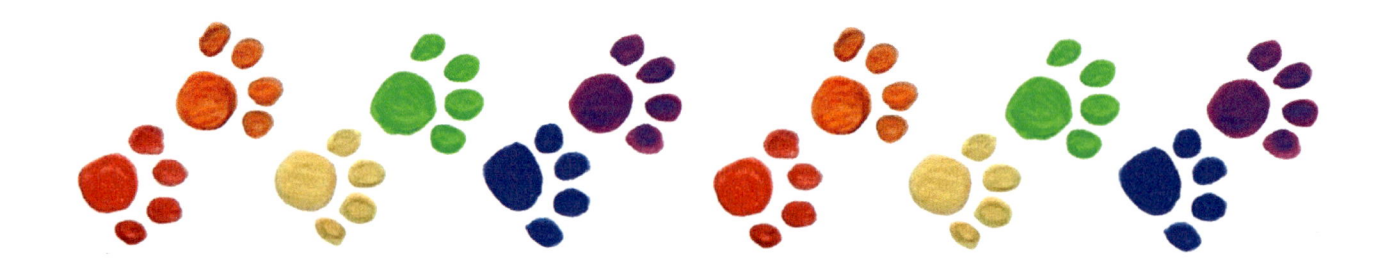

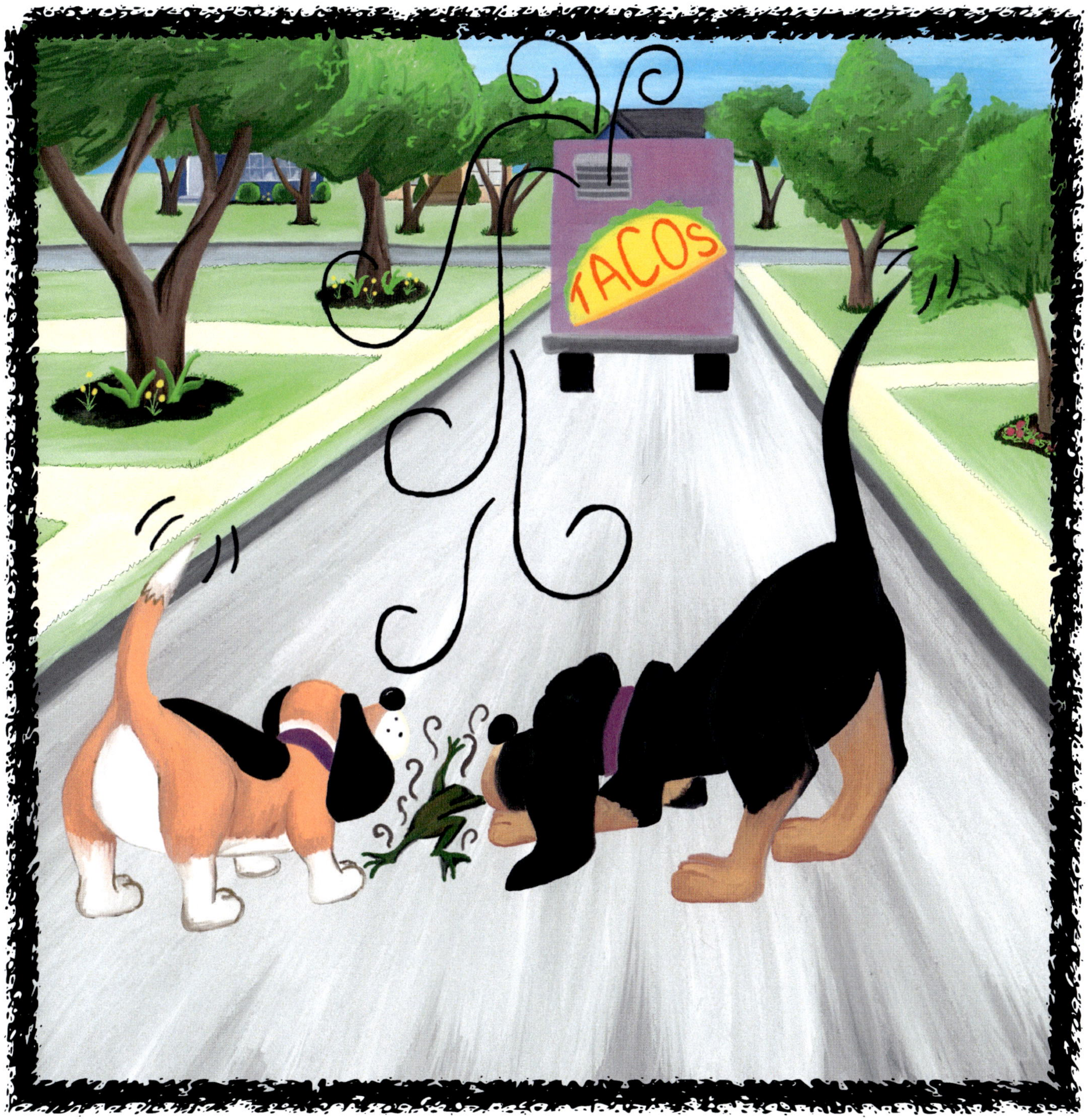
TACOS

While the dogs agreed that roadkill wasn't their taste, they didn't want to put its' amazing smell to waste.

They plopped down and rolled
in the middle of the street.
They smeared the roadkill toad
on their heads, backs and feet!

"We smell incredible!"
Tipsy let out a bay.
"Now back to taco tracking!
I think it went that way!"

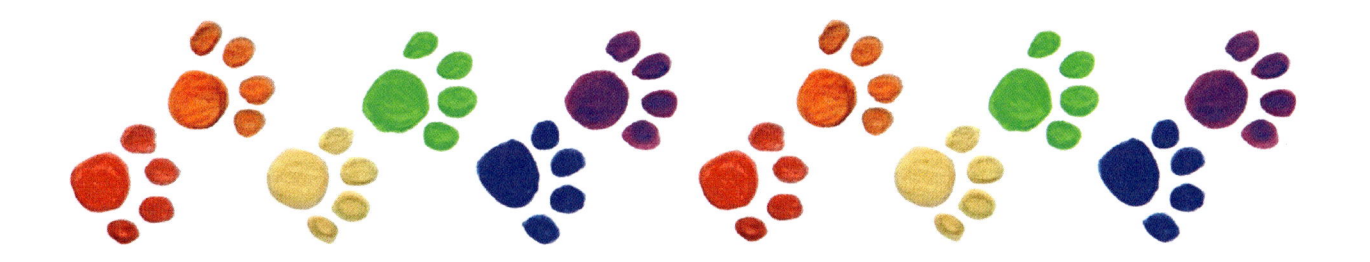

The hounds chased the scent of tacos...

and so much more...

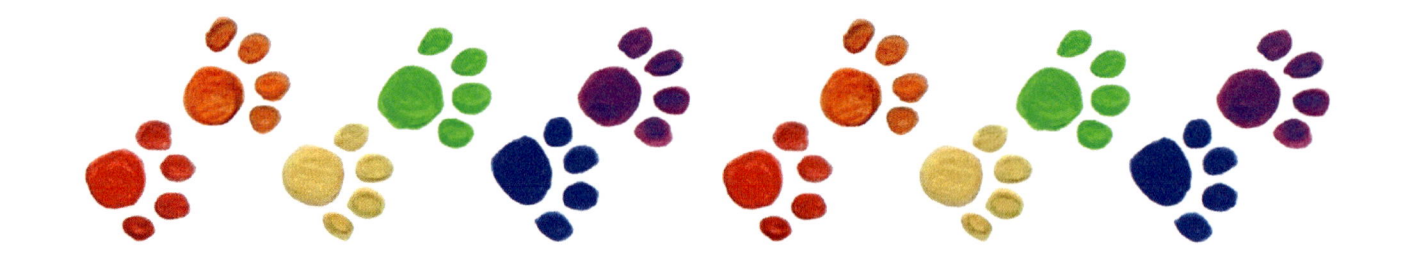

...until they found the truck
parked outside the grocery store.

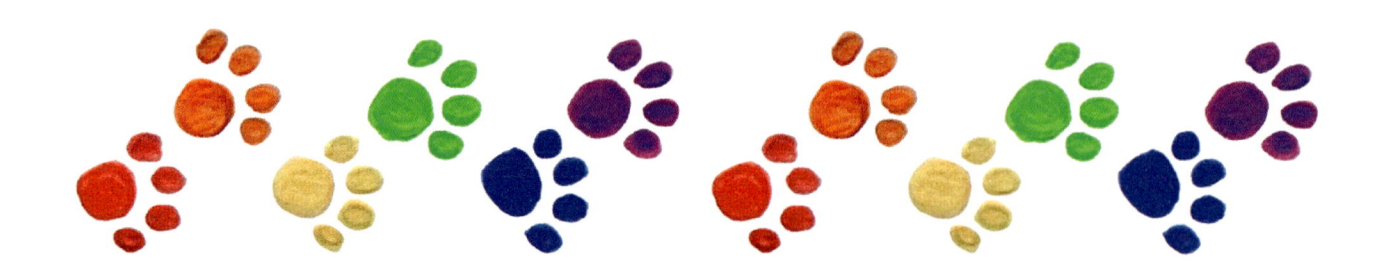

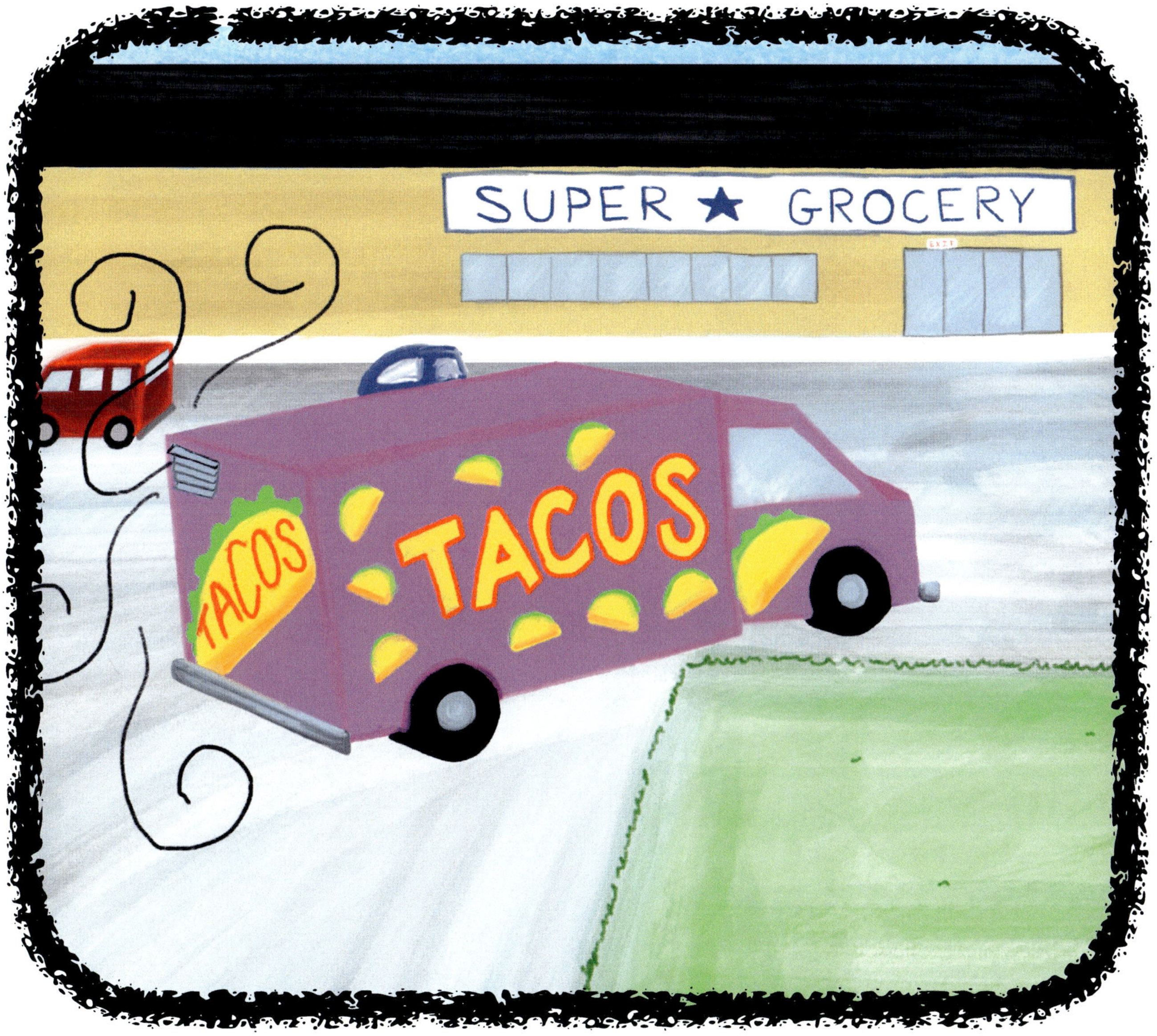
SUPER ★ GROCERY
TACOS
TACOS

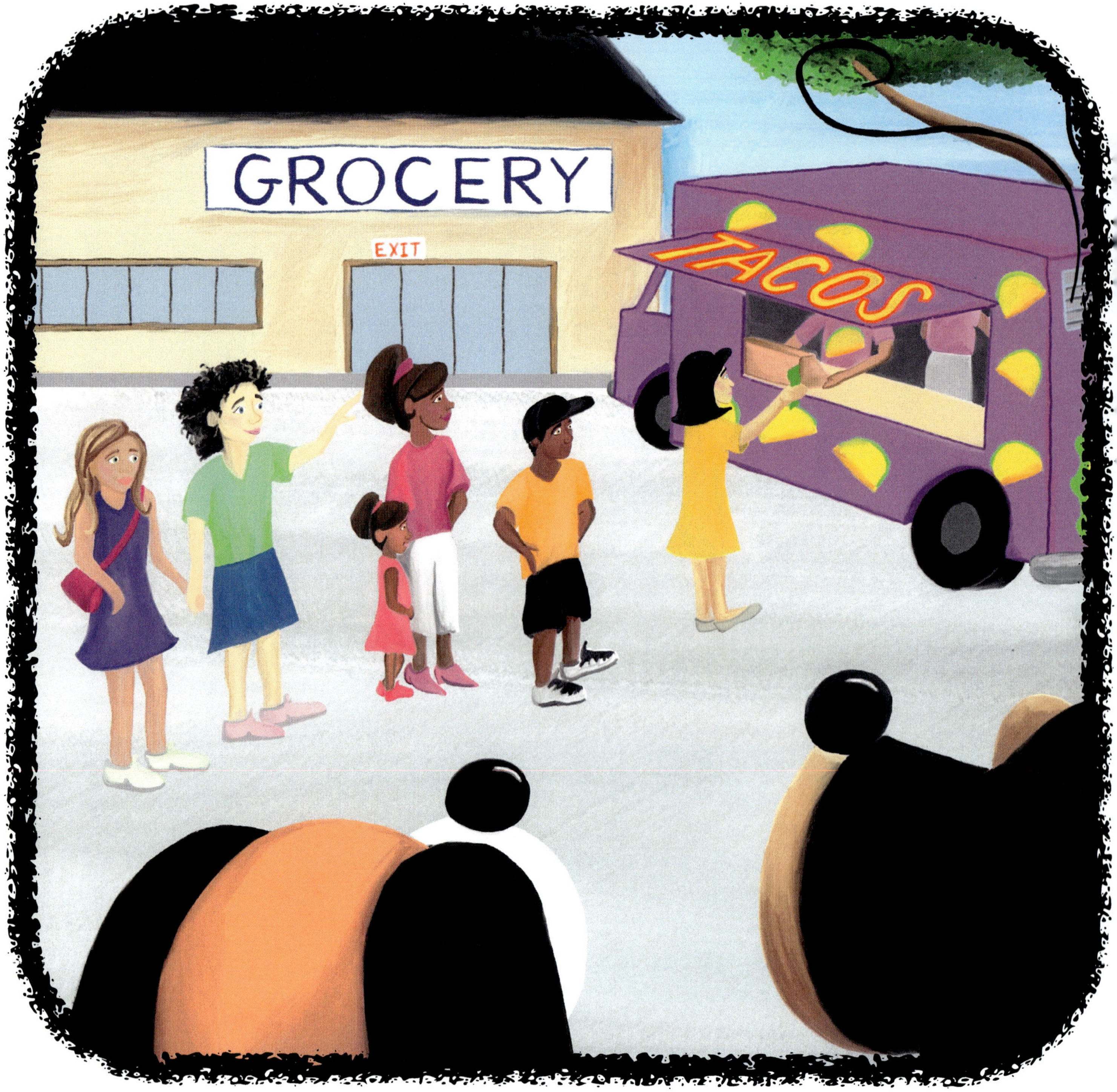
GROCERY
EXIT
TACOS

But the long line of customers
that the taco truck attracted
allowed for time and curiosity
to make the dogs distracted.

Tipsy asked, "do you mind if we take
a little, tiny detour?
I have a strong desire
to peek inside that store."

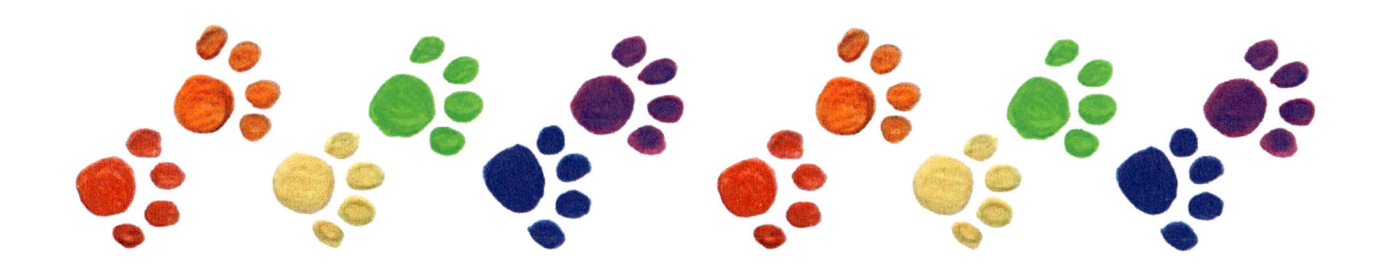

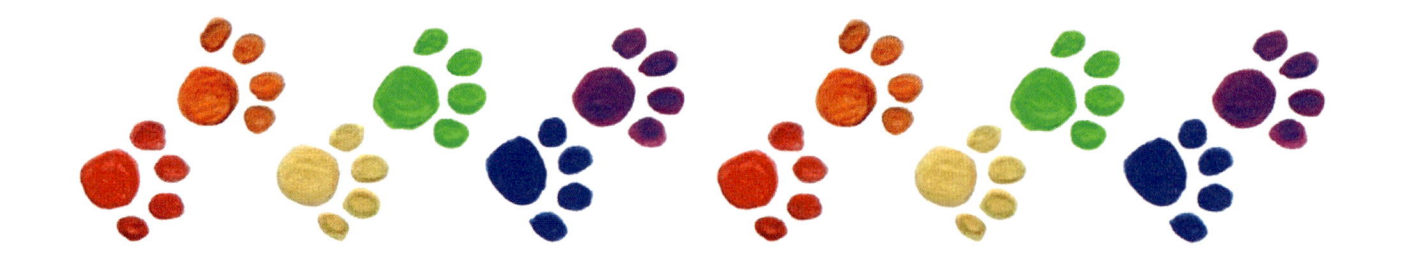

The hounds walked through the store,
isle by isle.
They passed by so many people
who didn't seem to smile.

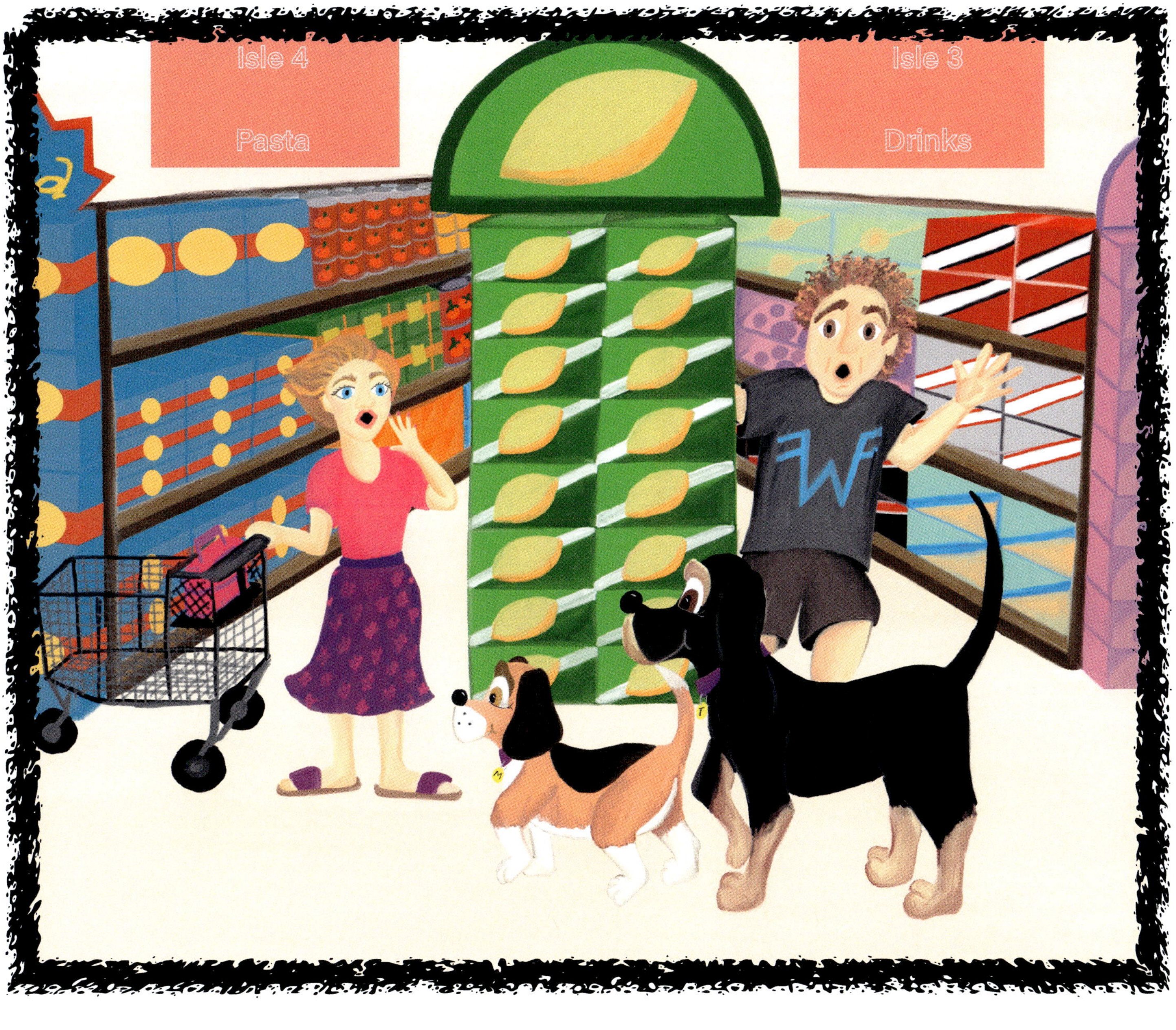

Isle 4
Pasta
Isle 3
Drinks

Isle 7
Pets
Beef
Beef
Beef
Small
Chicken
Chicken
Chicken
Organic
Medium
Lamb
Lamb
Lamb
Organic
Large
fetch!
chew!
catch!
tug!
squeak!

When the dogs finally came
to isle number seven,
they were pretty sure
that they had reached dog heaven.

There were bones high above
and bones near the floor.
Every shelf was filled with treats
and so much more!

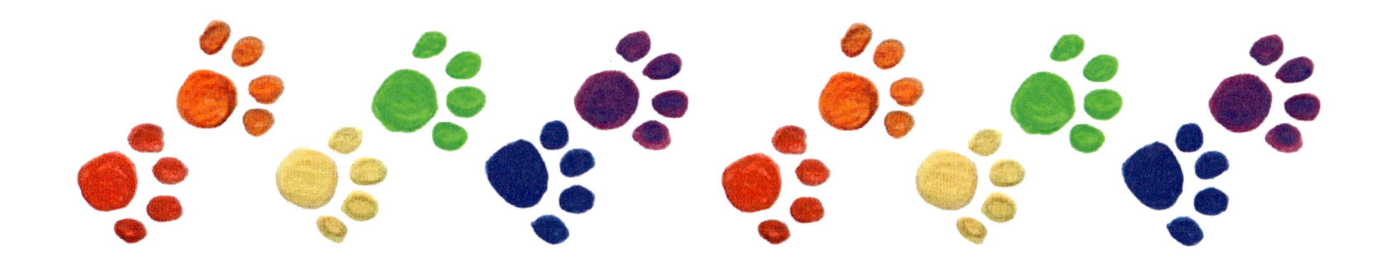

Mae howled, "grab a bag!
Let's fill it to the brim!"
Tipsy jumped and spun in circles,
dancing on hind limbs.

The dogs grabbed giant bones,
tasty treats and silly toys.
They filled a bag up
with all the things they would enjoy!

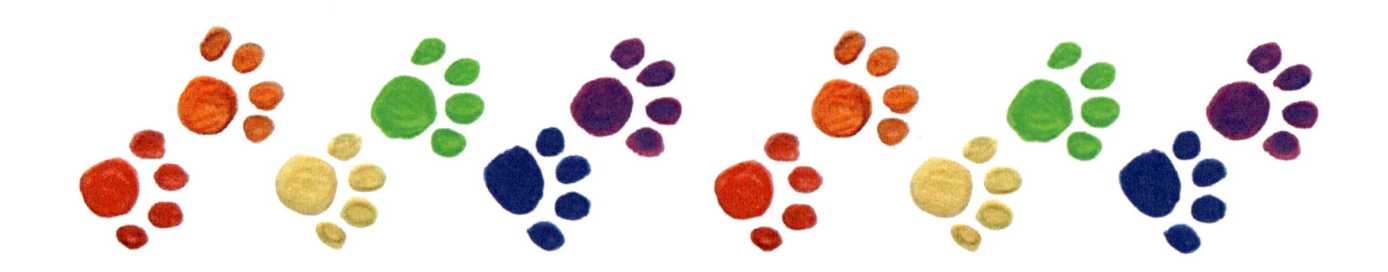

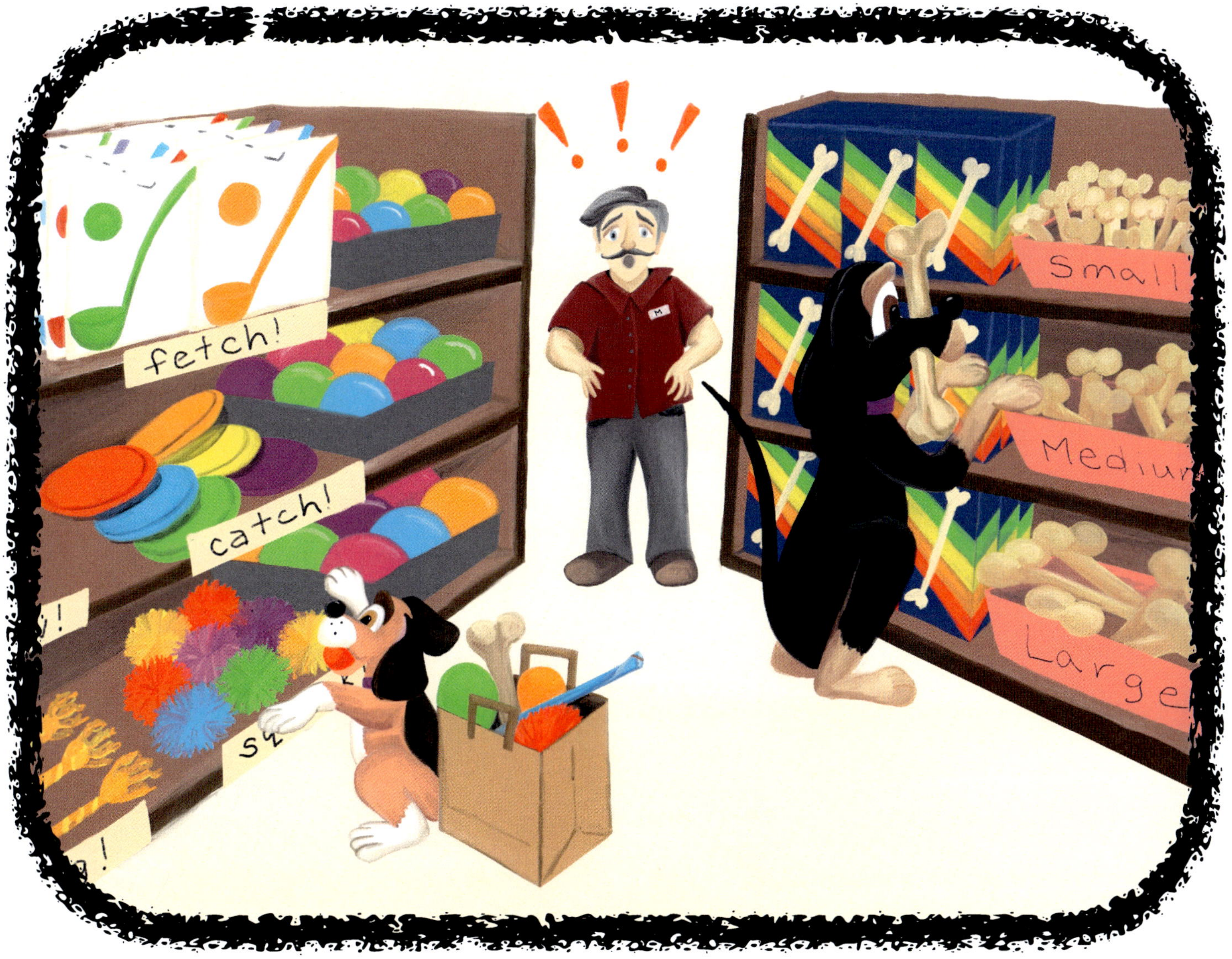
fetch!
catch!
Small
Large

They were just about to leave
with all their fancy loot
when the grocer grabbed their collars
and gave them the boot!

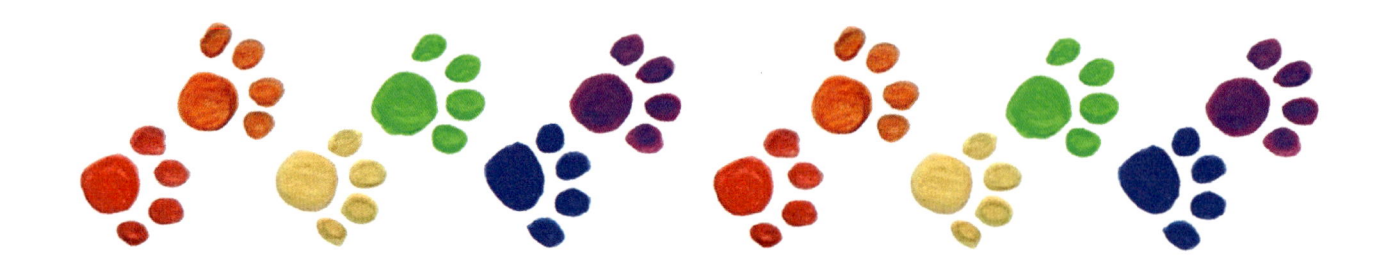

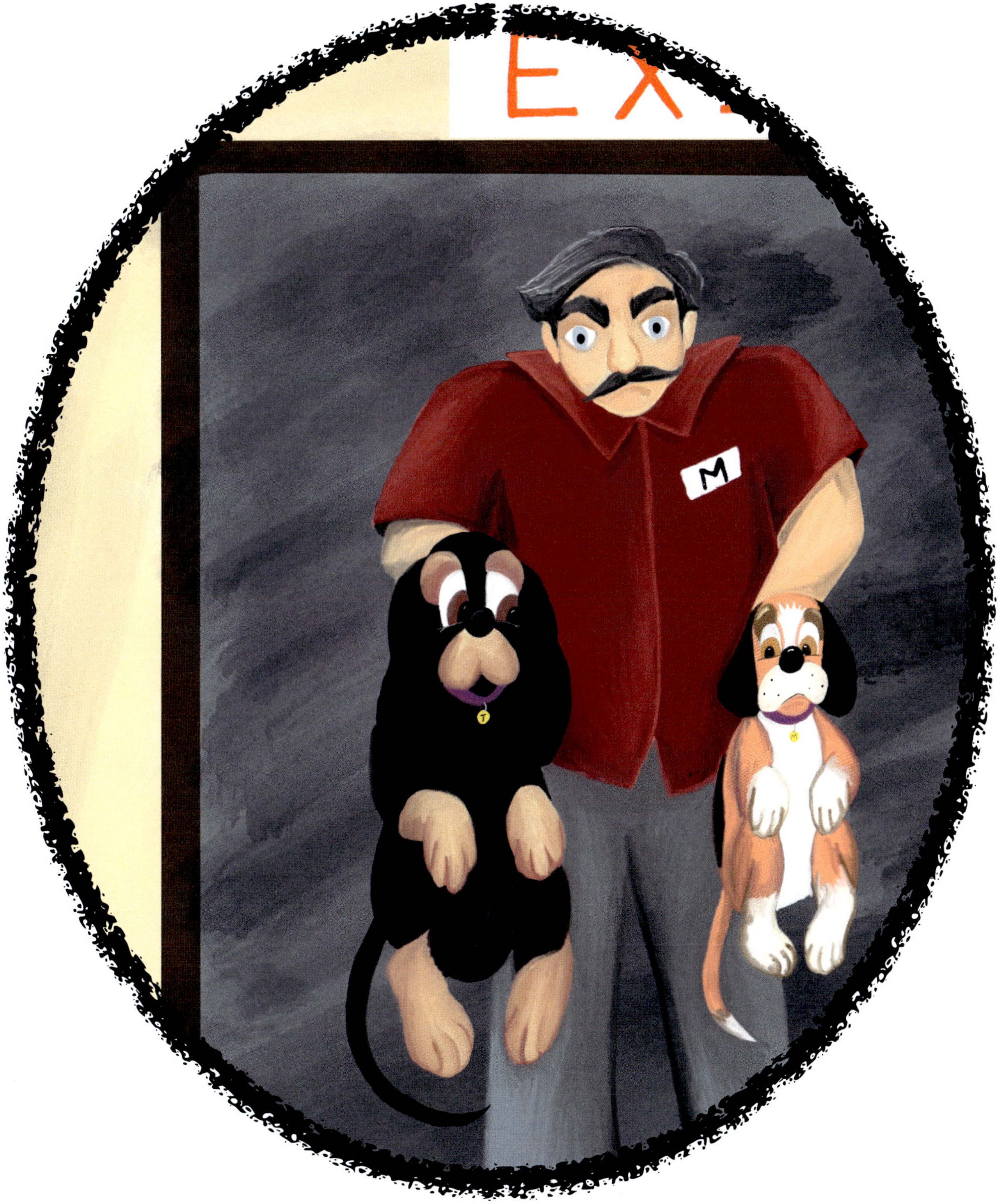
EX
M

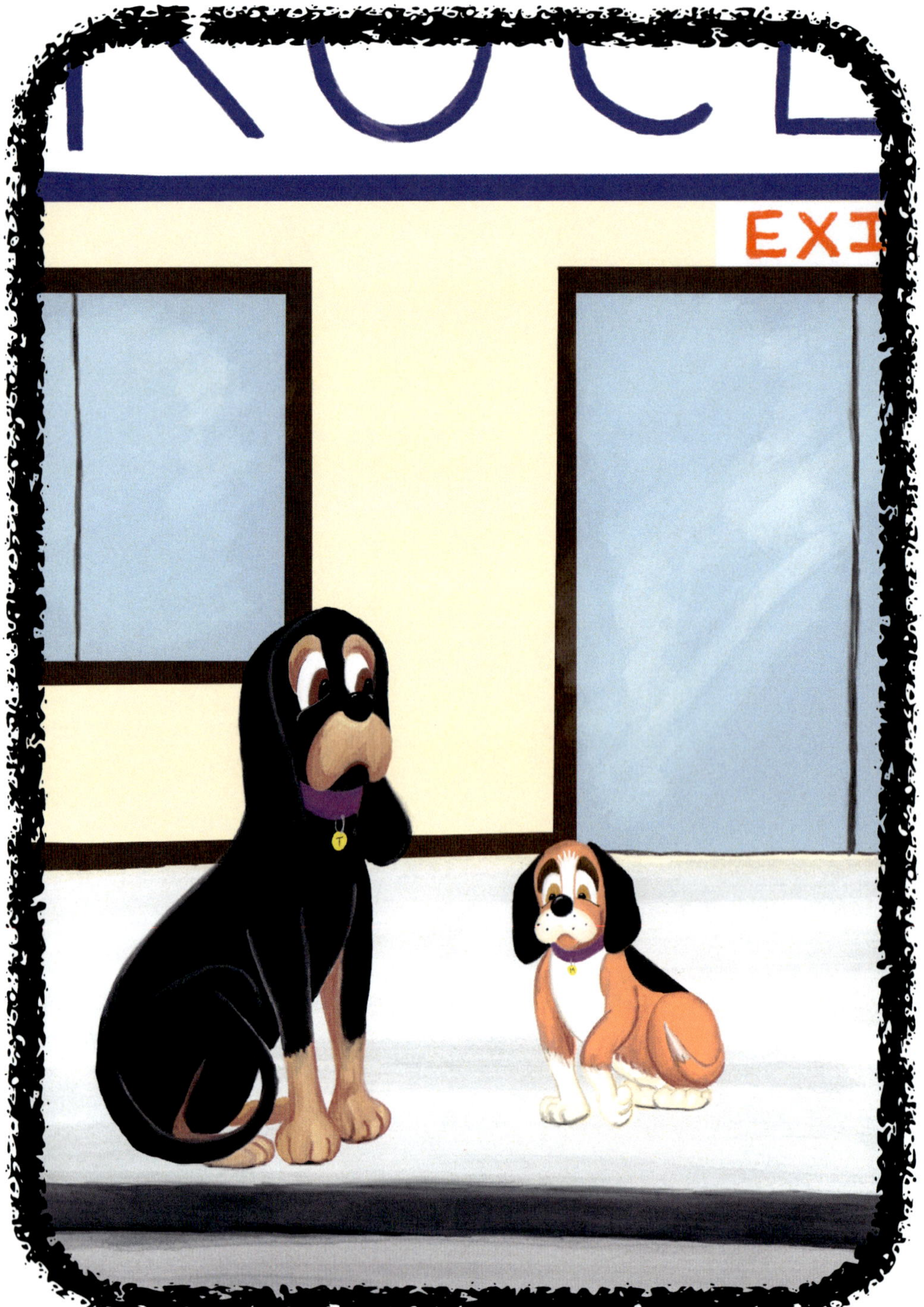
EXI

Tipsy sulked on the sidewalk,
"that was such bad luck.
We should've stayed focused
on the taco truck."

"But LOOK!" Mae exclaimed,
"I think our luck's about to swirl!
There's TWO tacos left
and they're with that little girl!"

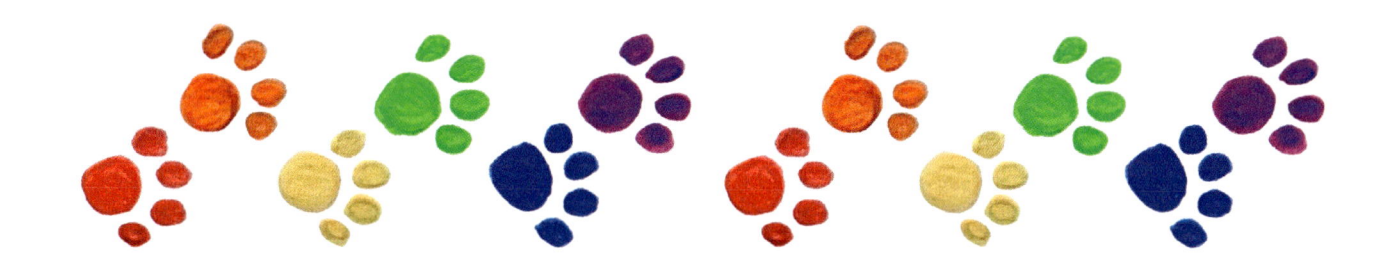

Sitting at a table
the girl began to munch,
while the dogs strategized
on how to take her lunch.

Mae sighed, "we can't just steal her lunch.
She'd cry and cause a scene."
Tipsy agreed, "it would also be rude
and incredibly mean."

"One thing is certain,
for us to get our wish,
we must act impossibly cute,
so the girl cannot resist."

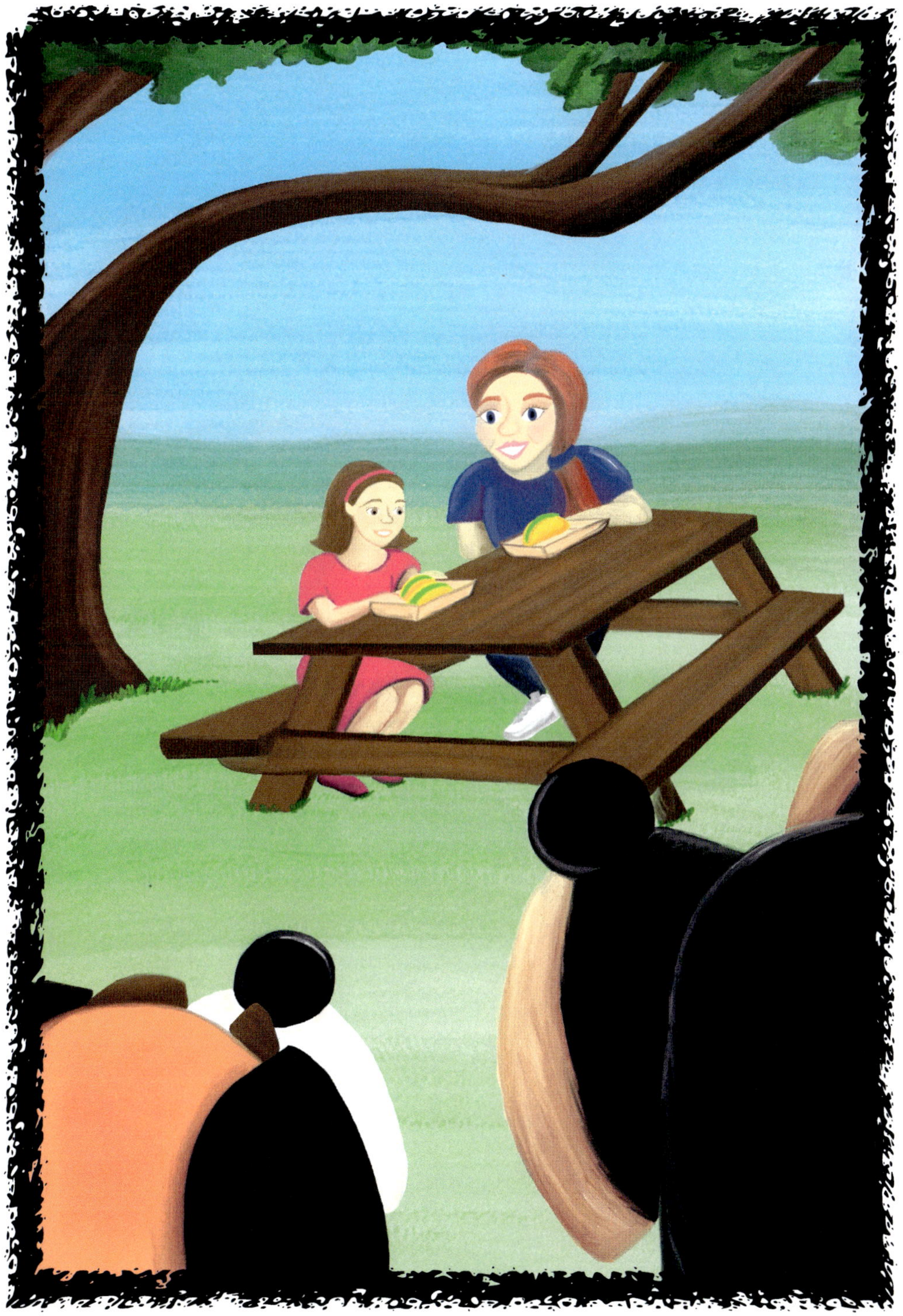

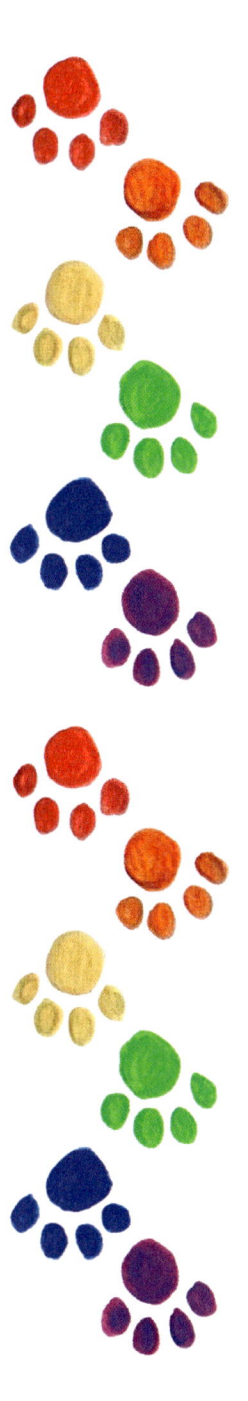

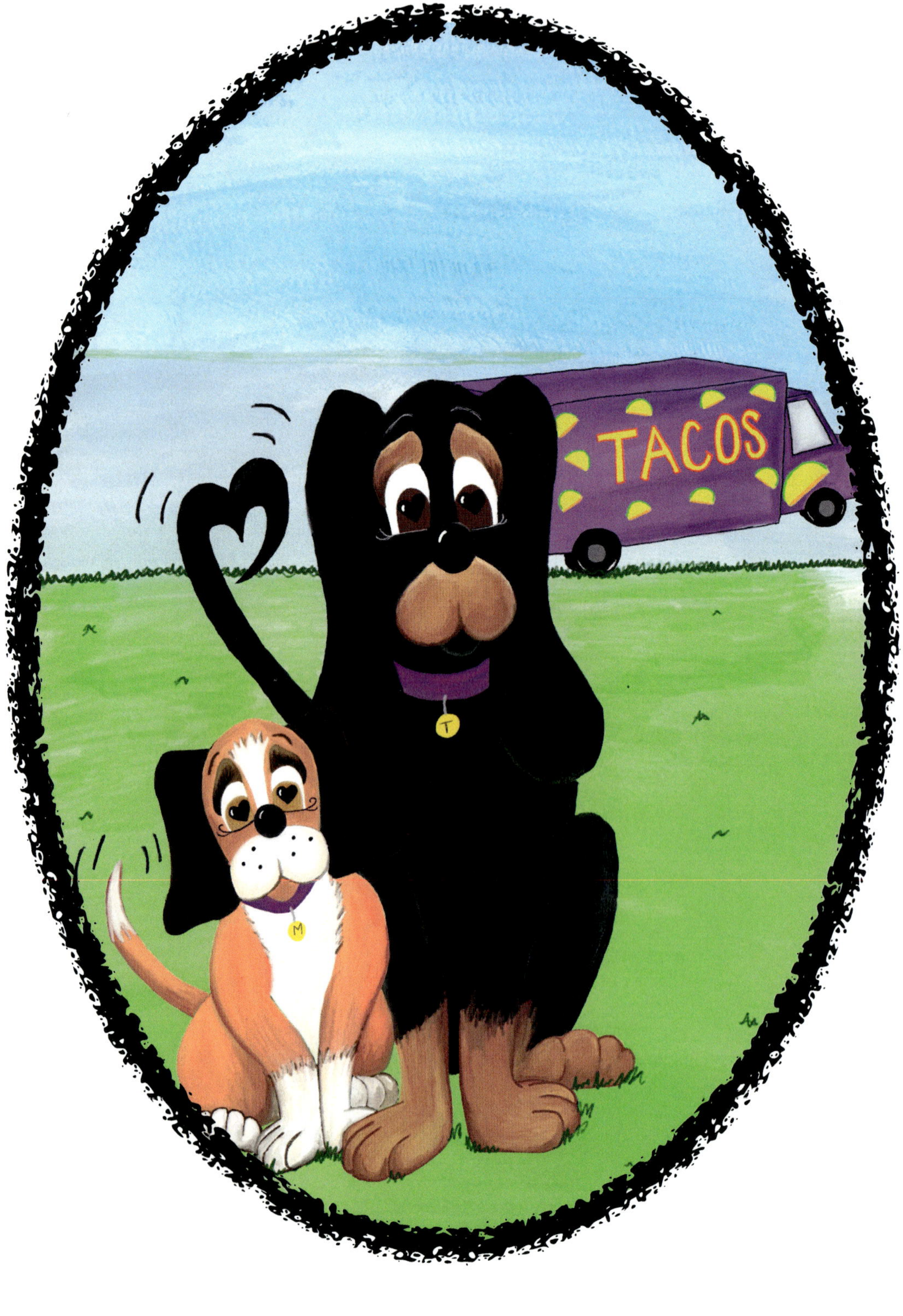
TACOS

The hounds walked to the table
and sat completely mute.
They perked their ears up,
wagged their tails and looked
SO cute!

They'd caught the girls attention.
She looked at them and smiled.
The hound's taco destiny
was in the hands of this dear child.

Patiently they watched her
savor every single bite,

and when she was too full
to eat the second taco...

the dogs salivated with delight!

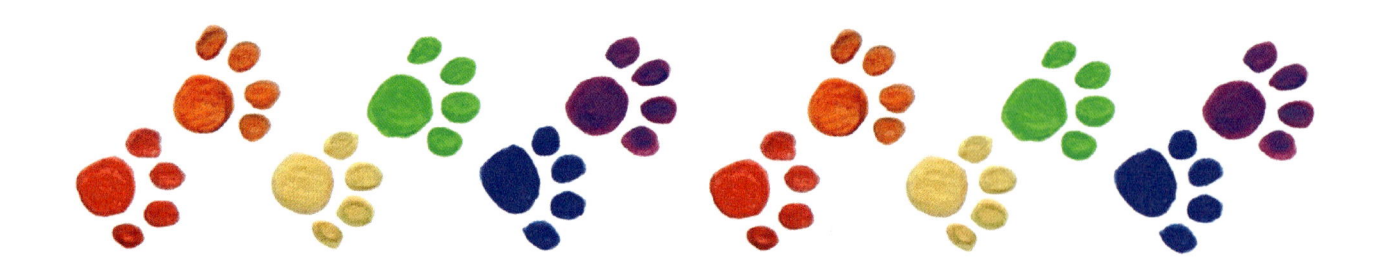

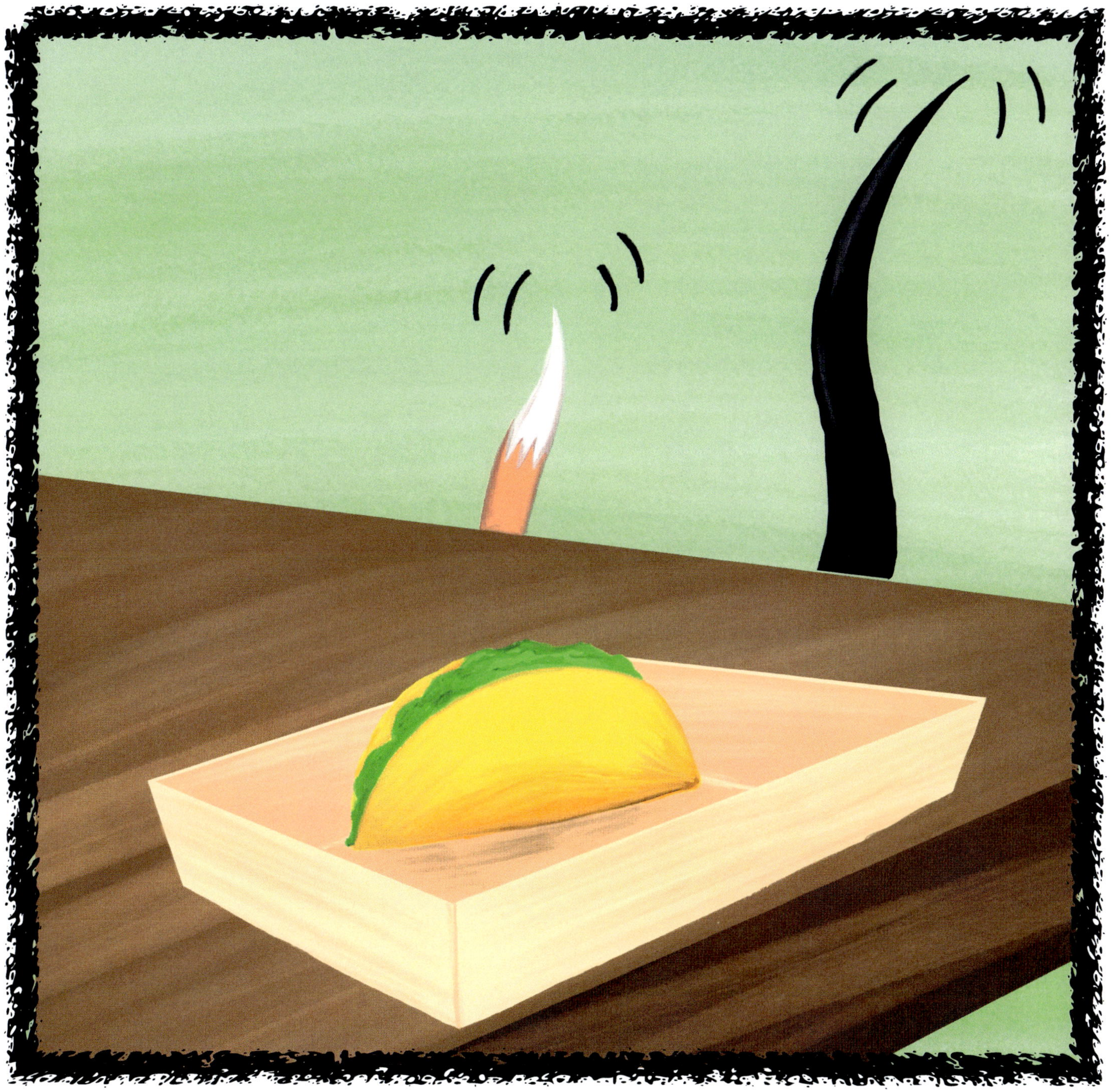

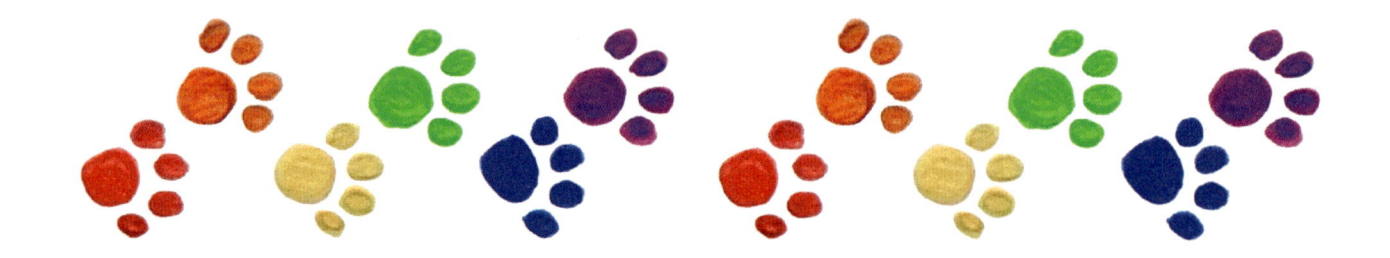

Tipsy and Mae Adventures

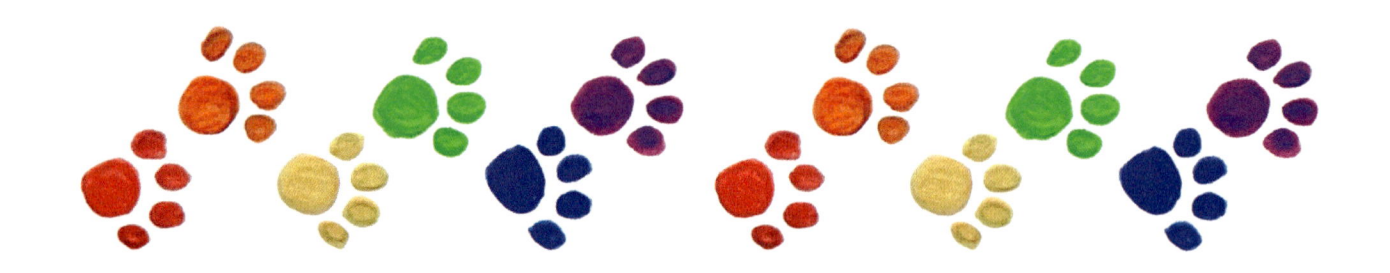

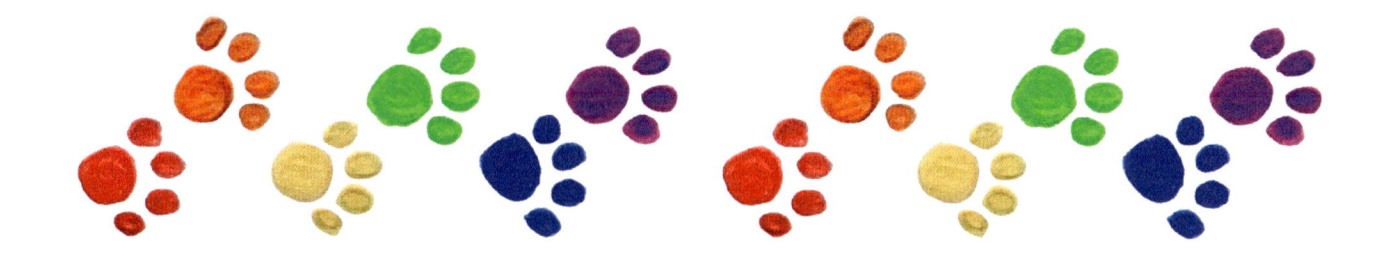

Tipsy is a black and tan coonhound.

Mae is a tri-color beagle.

They make loud howling sounds...**all the time!**

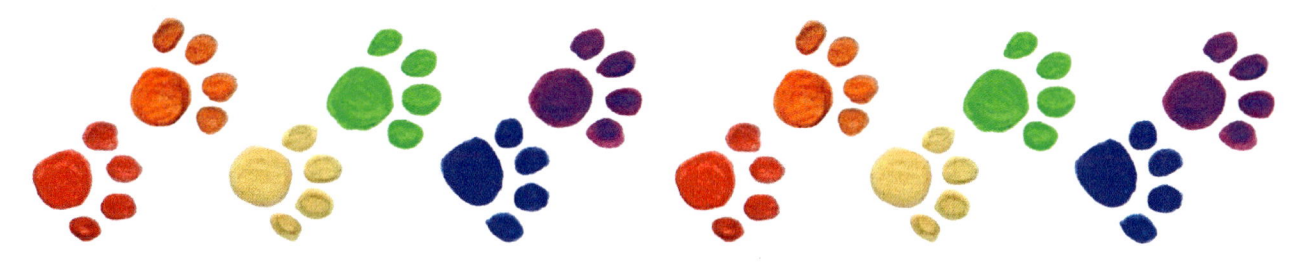

Kat Laxton has a Ph.D. in Curriculum and Instruction and her career has been primarily focused in science education. After nearly two decades of teaching, researching and writing in academics and public policy, Kat decided to transition her writing career into children's books. Kat lives in Seattle, WA with her husband, three children and two silly dogs,
Tipsy and Mae.

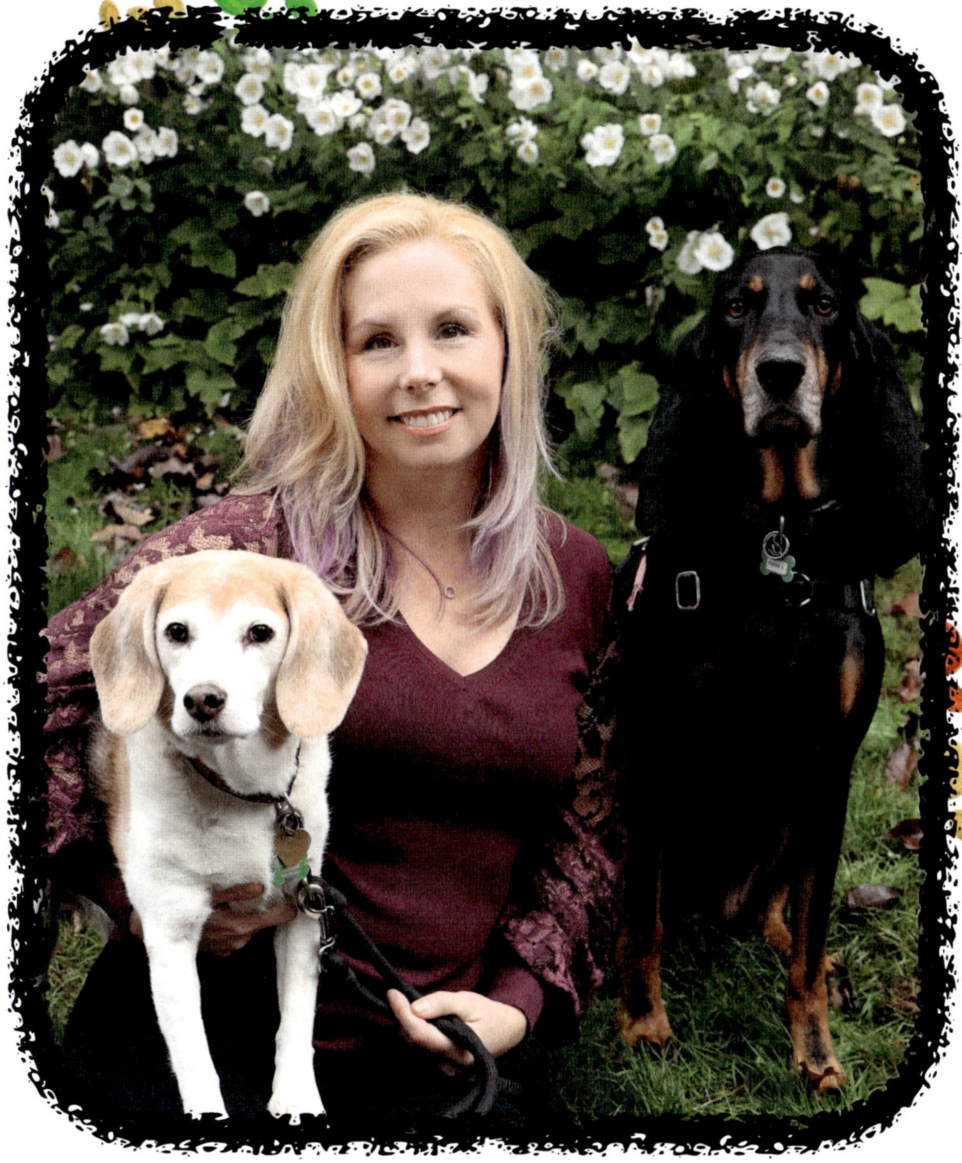

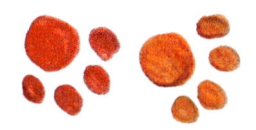

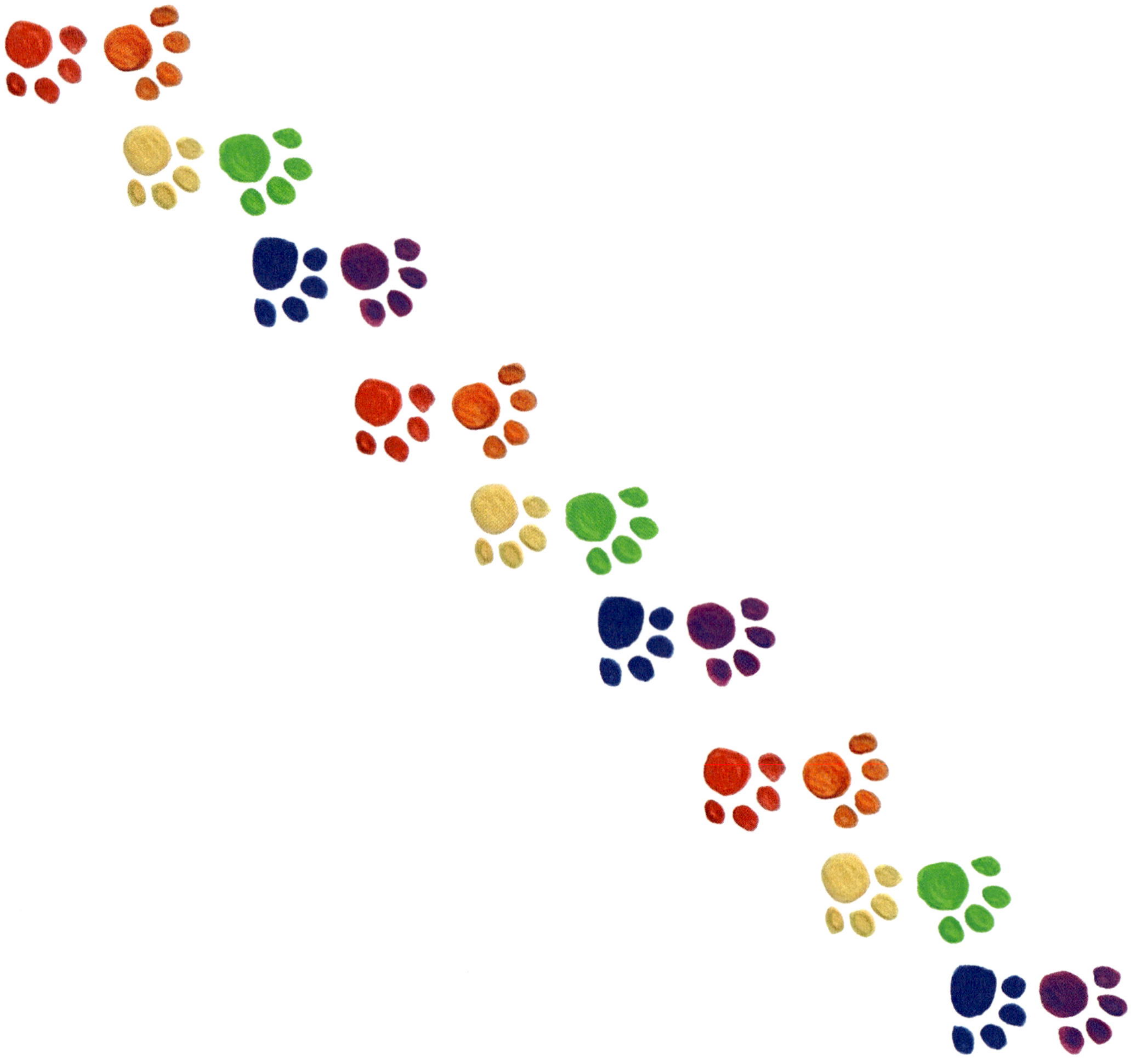

Acknowledgements

Thank you to everyone involved in helping me create this series. Most especially, thank you **Betty** for believing in me. Your unwavering enthusiasm and support helped me believe in myself. Thank you **Cathy** for sharing your wealth of experiential publishing knowledge and superb editing skills. Thank you **Carolyn** for being my sounding board, coach, reviewer, cheerleader and friend. Thank you **Karin** for encouraging me to pursue my passion. Thank you **Mark** for helping me become a better writer. Thank you **Drew** for being my rock and supporting me while I bring all of my crazy ideas to life. Thank you **EB, C & K** for all of our silly brainstorming sessions. Thank you **Tipsy** and **Mae** for being the hilarious beings that you are!

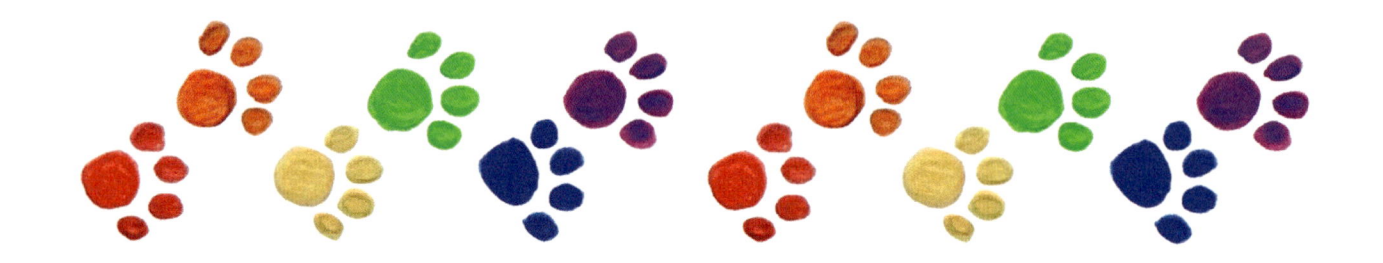

Check out more
Tipsy and Mae
Adventures!

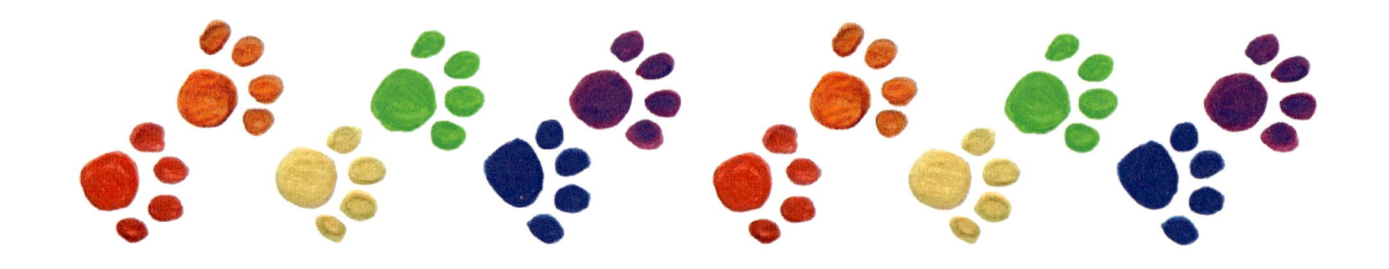

Follow us on Instagram!

@tipsymaeadventures

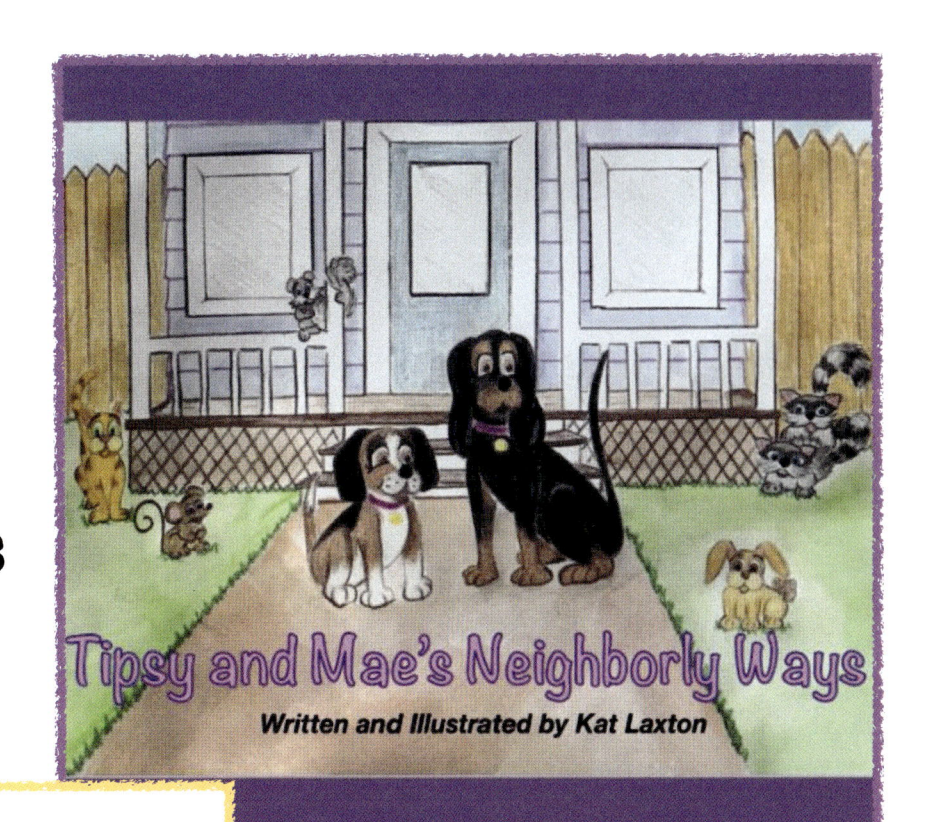

Made in United States
Orlando, FL
11 March 2022